A Break-of-Day Book®

Ever since 1928, when Wanda Gág's classic *Millions of Cats* appeared, Coward, McCann & Geoghegan has been publishing books of high quality for young readers. Among them are the easy-to-read stories known as Break-of-Day books. This series appears under the colophon shown above—a rooster crowing in the sunrise—which is adapted from one of Wanda Gág's illustrations for *Tales from Grimm*.

Though the language used in Break-of-Day books is deliberately kept as clear and as simple as possible, the stories are not written in a controlled vocabulary. And while chosen to be within the grasp of readers in the primary grades, their content is far-ranging and varied enough to captivate children who have just begun crossing the momentous threshold into the world of books.

YELLOW FUR
and LITTLE HAWK

by WILMA PITCHFORD HAYS
illustrated by ANTHONY RAO

COWARD, McCANN & GEOGHEGAN, INC.
NEW YORK

Library of Congress Cataloging in Publication Data

Hays, Wilma Pitchford.   Yellow Fur and Little Hawk.

(A Break-of-day book)
SUMMARY: A young girl living near a Sioux reservation in South
Dakota tries to find out why the Indians won't move into the new
homes built by her father.
[1. Dakota Indians—Fiction. 2. Indians of North America—
Fiction] I. Rao, Anthony. II. Title.
PZ7.H31493Ye   [Fic]   77-10712
ISBN 0-698-30687-2

CONTENTS

Chapter 1
Empty Houses

Susanna stood on the porch
with her Great Dane watchdog, Terk.
In the yard Papa talked with the
Agent-in-Charge of Indian Affairs.
The Agent said, "You build the houses.
I'll see that the Indians move in."
The Agent rode away.
Papa got on his horse
to ride to the Sioux village.
Susanna ran to him.
"Papa, are the Indians in trouble?"
she asked.
"They will be if they don't
move into the houses," Papa said.
"That's Government orders."

Susanna was worried.
Two houses had been built for the Sioux.
They stood empty. The Indians
lived right beside them in their tepees.
Papa smiled. "I'm finishing
White Bull's house today," he said.
"If he moves in, the others will.
White Bull's too smart
to let real trouble start for his people."
All day Susanna wondered
what White Bull would do
when Papa completed his house.
That afternoon she decided to find out.
She skipped through the prairie grass
on her way to the Sioux village,
singing words she often heard Mama sing.

    "Oh the doors they have no windows,
    and the windows have no panes,
    in my little old sod shanty on the plains."

She sang loudly, as she liked to sing
when no one could hear her.
    "We can hear the hungry coyotes,
    as they creep up through the grass,
    toward our little old sod shanty
    on the plains."
Two years before,
Susanna had come with Papa and Mama
to homestead near the Sioux reservation
in South Dakota.

She had made friends
with the Indians quickly.
At first Mama had been afraid of them.
Then she saw how much
Susanna liked the Indians,
and how much they liked her.
They called her "Yellow Fur"
because her hair was blond.
Now she visited the village often.
Papa had built such a strong house
for his own family that
the Agent-in-Charge of Indian Affairs
had hired him to build for the Sioux.
The United States Government planned
to move all Indians out of tepees
into frame houses
before winter winds came.

Susanna had heard the Agent tell Papa,
"They'll be warmer in houses—
and stay in one place.
I'll always know where they are."
Papa was on a ladder
hammering at the door of the new house.
White Bull sat nearby under a shelter
made of pine posts
roofed with brown pine boughs.
Sioux men had brought the pines
from a long distance
to shade the old Indian from the hot sun.
There were no trees on the prairie.
Even the lumber for the houses
had to be brought by horse and wagon,
a three-day trip from the nearest town.

No wonder the Indians
had always made their rounded tepees
of tanned buffalo hide,
Susanna thought.
The old Indian wasn't watching Papa.
He wasn't looking at anything.
White Bull seems sad, Susanna thought.
Why isn't he happy to have a new house?
White Bull was one of
the old "long-hairs."
He was a *wich-as-ha wa-kon*, a holy man,
important among the Sioux.
He taught their people
the things that were right to do.
He had told Susanna
and his grandson, Little Hawk,
stories about Sioux heroes.
In two years Susanna had learned
to understand the Sioux language well,
and to speak it a little.
She stopped in front of White Bull.
"Are you going to move
into your new house tonight?" she asked.
He was smoking a pipe and did not answer.

She waited.
He sometimes thought a long time
before he answered.
"Hot," he said at last.
"Better sleep here in the air."
Susanna lifted the damp blond curls
from her neck.

The sun had been hot for days.
Sap oozed from knotholes
in the fresh lumber of the house.
"It has a wonderful piney woods smell,"
she said to Papa.
He came down the ladder
and stood before White Bull.
"Your house is ready," he said, smiling.
"No stove in yet.
Don't think you'll need one right away."
"No," White Bull said too politely.
Papa waited a minute.
He saw that White Bull wasn't going
to say anything more.

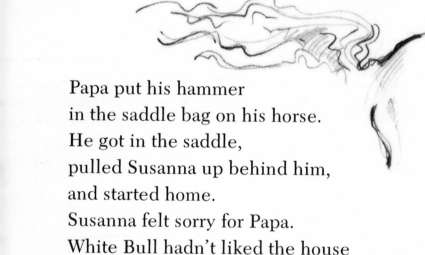

Papa put his hammer
in the saddle bag on his horse.
He got in the saddle,
pulled Susanna up behind him,
and started home.
Susanna felt sorry for Papa.
White Bull hadn't liked the house
that Papa had worked so hard to build.
"Why won't the Indians
live in the houses?" she asked.
"I wish I knew," Papa said.
"They wouldn't disobey
a Government order
without some reason."

Susanna didn't feel like
asking White Bull.
But she was a good friend
of his grandson, Little Hawk.
And White Bull had begun
to teach the boy
all the things he knew.
"Tomorrow," she said,
"I'll ask Little Hawk."

Chapter 2
Sioux Ways

Susanna went to the Sioux village early.
Terk tried to follow her.
"Stay home," she told him.
He whined and took
one more step, begging.
"No," she said.
"You'll get hot and need water.
The Indians are as short of water
as we are."
She always talked to him
as if he understood.
He went back and lay down
under the shade of the porch,
his jaws on his front paws.
Susanna could see a long way
across the treeless low hills.
White Bull was sitting under the shelter
beside his tepee.
She was glad to see
Little Hawk there, too.

He sat on the ground
in front of the old man.
Indian children
had no real school or teachers.
The girls and boys
learned Sioux ways from everyone.
They tried to do the things
the men and women of their village
did best—riding horseback,
shooting a bow and arrow,
cooking over a campfire,
and tanning leather and embroidering it.
They learned how
to make plans for their tribe,
by listening to men and women
talk in council.

They joined in celebrations,
dancing and singing old songs,
telling stories.
Once in a while a *wich-as-ha wa-kon*
chose to teach one girl or boy
all the sacred things that he knew.
White Bull had chosen his grandson.
Every day Little Hawk
listened to the old man for an hour or two.
Susanna came to them now
and sat down, quietly.
They paid no attention to her.

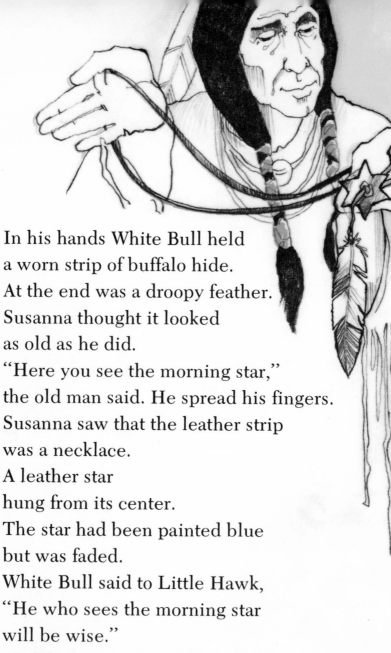

In his hands White Bull held
a worn strip of buffalo hide.
At the end was a droopy feather.
Susanna thought it looked
as old as he did.
"Here you see the morning star,"
the old man said. He spread his fingers.
Susanna saw that the leather strip
was a necklace.
A leather star
hung from its center.
The star had been painted blue
but was faded.
White Bull said to Little Hawk,
"He who sees the morning star
will be wise."
He lifted the strip of hide.
"This means all the good things
in the world," he said.

"Our tepees are made of buffalo hide,
and the buffalo gave us food."
He touched the eagle feather.
"This reminds us of Wakon Tonka,
the Great Mysterious One.
The feather tells us
our thoughts must rise high-high
as the eagles do."
Susanna knew Wakon Tonka
was the Sioux word for God.
"My grandson," White Bull said,
"I had these things.
I wish them *all* for you.
Take my necklace.
Wear it around your neck,
and remember."
Susanna didn't move.
She watched the boy
put the leather loop over his head.

He stood up and smiled at her.
"Yellow Fur," he said.
"Come. Watch the heyokas perform."
Susanna and Little Hawk
walked through a circle of tepees.
Indians had gathered
in the center of the yard.
"Hey-a-hey," men called.
"Hey-a-hey," women sang.
"Hey-hey-hey-a-hey," children shouted.
They clapped, keeping time to their cries.
"Behold! Heyokas, they come!
Laughing they come.
Make us laugh!"
Susanna knew that the heyoka
was a special kind of man
among the Sioux.
A heyoka did everything backward.

He must walk backward,
ride backward on a horse.
If others laughed,
he must cry to remind them
of those people who were sad.
If the tribe was in trouble,
he must act silly
to make people laugh and feel better.
Today two heyokas
were in the circle
doing foolish tricks.

"What's the matter?"
Susanna asked Little Hawk.
"What's worrying the people?"
Little Hawk was laughing
too hard to answer.
One heyoka had painted his body red.
Yellow zigzags of lightning
were streaked down his back.
The other man was painted yellow
with black zigzags.

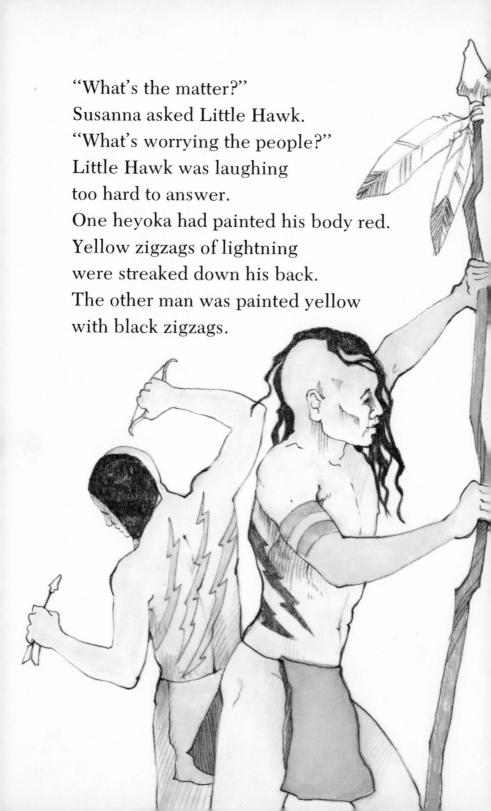

Both of them had shaved their heads
on one side. On the other side,
their hair hung long and black.
The red man carried a tiny bow and arrow,
too small for the youngest child.
The yellow man held
a great crooked arrow,
so long he kept tripping over it.
They pretended to fight each other,
falling down, rolling in the dust.
The people took sides,
shouting for the red or the yellow to win.
The red man drew his tiny bow.
The yellow man tripped,
fell on his knees,
begged for his life.
Everyone was laughing.
Susanna had to laugh, too.
She shouted "Hey-a-hey" and clapped.
"They're like clowns,"
she told Little Hawk.
"But why are they
acting this backward happy way today?"
"Because the creek is dry," he said.

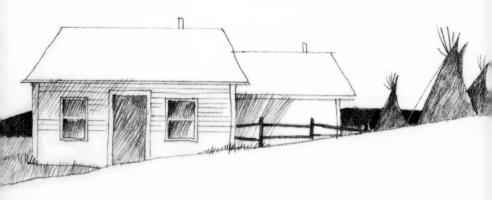

"The heyokas act funny
to make us forget that we are thirsty."
Susanna nodded.
"We don't have much water
at home, either," she said.
Little Hawk's older sister
came and spoke to Susanna.
"You do not wear
the Sioux dress we made for you,
Yellow Fur, or the moccasins."
Susanna stuck out one foot.
"I'm too big for them now," she said.
"But they are so pretty,

Mama hung them on the wall
like a picture."
The girl smiled, pleased.
The heyoka ceremony was over.
Susanna and Little Hawk
walked past the empty new houses.
Susanna asked,
"Did your grandfather tell you
why he won't move into his house?"
"No," Little Hawk said.
"Maybe he thinks it is
a little coop for chickens.
It's only a little bigger
than his tepee.
And it has no picture stories
painted on it, as tepees have."

At supper she told her family
what Little Hawk had said.
"The Indians are stubborn," Mama said.
"When they want to do something—
or don't want to do something—
no one can change their minds."
Susanna's little brother
beat on the table with his spoon
as if he agreed with her.
He did not talk yet.
Susanna did not think Mama was right.
"The Indians are my friends," she said.
"I don't want them to get into trouble."

Papa said, "Little Hawk's reasons
don't seem important enough
to disobey the Indian Agent's orders.
The Agent is right about one thing.
A house is greater protection
against wind and hail and blizzard."
"Maybe they'd like the houses better,"
Susanna suggested,
"if they painted pictures on them."
Papa smiled at that.
"They can do anything they want," he said,
"as long as they move in."

Chapter 3
Water from the Smoky Earth River

For a week the sun was so hot
that Mama told Susanna
not to leave the shade of the porch.
Each day the windmill turned and creaked,
turned and creaked.
No water came.
The well under it had gone dry.
Susanna and Mama
tied on their checked sunbonnets
and walked to the creek for water.
It was dry.
Its bed was cracked into little clay curls
that crunched under their feet.
They knew there was one deeper hole
under a dried grassy bank.
They dipped their pails
into a few inches of muddy water.
Mama had brought a white cloth.
She strained the gray liquid through it.

Three small snakes
slid over the edge of the pail,
back into the waterhole.
Mama shuddered.
Susanna said, "It's the only place
snakes can find water, too."
In the kitchen Mama boiled the water
and strained it again.
Susanna was very, very thirsty.
Finally she sipped a little of it.
It tasted of mud and frogs.
Papa came in from the barn.
"If we don't get rain today," he said,
"we'll have to go
to the White River for water.
The horses won't drink that scum
from the waterhole in the creek."
That evening a small cloud
moved across the setting sun.
The family sat on the porch
and watched it anxiously.
"I thought I heard thunder,"
Susanna said hopefully.

Terk stood up slowly
as if he had heard something too.
He had scarcely moved
from the shade of the porch
the last few days.
He was a big dog,
so big the Indians called him
"Dog-Big-as-a-Pony."
He needed more water
than they had for him.
Everyone sniffed for the smell of rain.
But the air was dry as dust.

"We'll leave for the river
before daylight tomorrow,"
Papa said at last.
Once, two years ago, they had gone
to the White River
and brought water home in barrels.
"How many barrels
will our wagon hold?" she asked.
"Eight will fill it," Papa said.
"You'll have to sit on one of them."
Papa waked her from sleep
before he went to hitch up the horses.

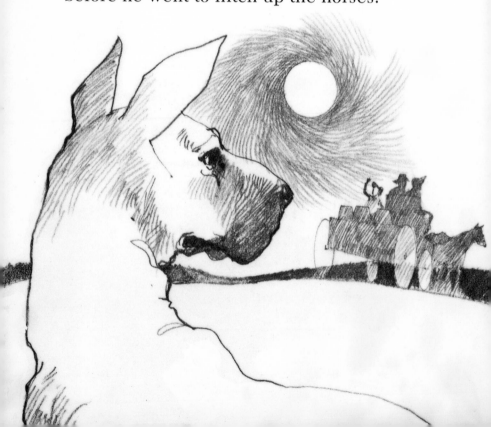

She dressed quickly and tied on
her red-and-white checked sunbonnet.
She helped Mama carry
packets of sandwiches and cookies
to the wagon.
Luckily the moon was full
and gave a good half-light.
Brother couldn't wake up.
Mama held him on her lap
as she sat on the spring seat beside Papa.
Susanna poured the last of the creek water
into a pan for Terk,
before she climbed up on the barrels.
Terk tried to follow them
but Papa sent him back.
"There's no room for you, Terk,"
Susanna called. "And you can't
walk all that way.
We'll bring you water."
By midmorning the sun was so hot
that Mama told Susanna to squeeze
into the seat beside her.
Mama opened her parasol
and held it over their heads.

They all sang together.
Papa had a wonderful voice.
When he sang "Perfect Day,"
she could almost believe it was.
They sang "Shall We Gather at the River"
and "My Old Sod Shanty on the Plains."
"We're like the heyokas," Susanna said.
"It's fun to sing,
so we forget we're hot."
When they reached the White River,
a dozen Sioux men were there
with a string of horses.
Each horse carried two skin saddlebags
filled with water
to take back to the village.
Papa spoke to Little Hawk's father.

Susanna heard the Indian say,
"We can't carry enough water
for the people.
In the old days
our whole village moved here in summer.
Now the Agent says
no tepees here."
After he had gone, Susanna said to Papa,
"Maybe that's why Indians like tepees.
They can take them down
and move them wherever there is
food and water.
You can't do that with a house."
"They aren't allowed
to move villages anymore," Papa said.
It's against Agency rules."

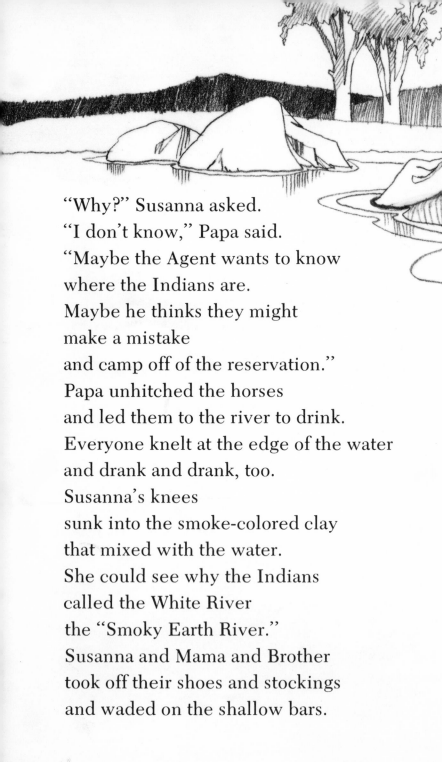

"Why?" Susanna asked.
"I don't know," Papa said.
"Maybe the Agent wants to know
where the Indians are.
Maybe he thinks they might
make a mistake
and camp off of the reservation."
Papa unhitched the horses
and led them to the river to drink.
Everyone knelt at the edge of the water
and drank and drank, too.
Susanna's knees
sunk into the smoke-colored clay
that mixed with the water.
She could see why the Indians
called the White River
the "Smoky Earth River."
Susanna and Mama and Brother
took off their shoes and stockings
and waded on the shallow bars.

40

They dipped their hands
and splashed one another.
Mama didn't say a word
about keeping their clothes dry,
so they lay down and soaked—
clothes and all.
The horses rested.
The family ate their lunch
under a cottonwood tree.
Then Papa hitched up the team
and backed the wagon into the river.
He got out and stood in waist-deep water.
He lifted pails of water
until he had filled all the barrels.
They started home.
"I'd hate to lift that much water again,"
he said. "Rain had better come soon."

Chapter 4
Where's Terk?

They reached home about midnight.
Mama took Brother right in to bed.
Susanna ran to the porch
where Terk slept.
"Terk," she called.
"We brought you water."
No bark answered her.
He did not come.
She felt in the dark for his bed.
"Terk's gone," she called.
She ran around the house, calling for him.
Papa lighted a kerosene lantern.
They saw that his water pan was empty.
"He was so thirsty," Susanna said.
"He went to hunt water."
She was afraid he might die
out on the dry prairie.
"We have to hunt him," she said.
"Maybe he went to the Indians."
"I hope so," Papa said.
"They'll look after him until we come."

"Can't we go and see?" she asked.
"Not until morning," Papa said.
"The horses can't
move another step tonight—
neither can I."
Susanna wakened at sunup.
Papa had already
hitched the horses to the wagon.
He had left one barrel of water in it
to take to White Bull.
Susanna went with him
to see if Terk was there.
White Bull sat under the shelter
beside his tepee.
Papa stopped the horses in front of him,
got out of the wagon,
and let down the tailgate.

Two Indian men saw the heavy barrel.
They came to help lift it under the shelter.
They stood back then,
but they did not go away.
They were very thirsty, too.
Papa handed a dipper of water
to White Bull.
The men dipped water
in their cupped hands and drank.
They started to drink slowly,
to be polite,
but the water was gone in a minute.
"My friend," White Bull said to Papa.
"We are grateful."

Susanna had waited long enough.
"Have you seen Terk?" she said.
The old Indian nodded.
"He came. Hot and weak. We had no water.
We tied him to the new house
to keep him for you.
He pulled loose. He is gone."
"Oh, where?" Susanna said.
"Little Hawk
is looking for him," White Bull said.
"He will go to every waterhole."

Susanna knew the waterholes were dry.
She blinked hard not to cry.
Papa said, "I'll ride
one of the horses to find Terk.
You wait here, Susanna."
Papa left.
Susanna sat on the ground
under the shelter
and pushed back
her red-and-white checked sunbonnet.
For a long time the old man sat
and sipped water from the dipper.
He said nothing.
Susanna looked at
the empty new house beside them.
Its front door had been torn off.
She said, "Papa made such a nice door."
The old Indian nodded.
"Did someone take the door
for a cooking fire?" she asked.
He lifted his shoulders.
Maybe he knew. Maybe he didn't.
"They will break up all the house,"
she said.

"Why won't you live in it, White Bull?"
He looked at her without speaking.
Susanna knew he was deciding something.
Should he tell her these things
that belonged only to the Sioux?
At last he said,
"Indians live in a circle.
The Mysterious One,
Power of the World,
made nature in a circle.
The sun is round, and the moon.
The earth and the sky.
Sioux have always
made their tepees round
like the nests of birds.
Tepees are set in a circle, too.

We cannot live in a square box."
Susanna said in surprise,
"You *did* have a reason
not to live in the houses.
Why didn't you say so?"
"No one asked us," he said.
Little Hawk came around the house.
"Yellow Fur," he called.
Susanna jumped up.
"Did you find Terk?" she cried.
"He's across the prairie
at a buffalo wallow," he said,
"where water used to be."
"Why didn't you bring him?" she asked.
"He lies there, too weak to walk.
Too heavy to carry," Little Hawk said.

"If we had water—"
"We'll take him some," Susanna said.
Little Hawk saw the barrel.
White Bull handed him the dipper.
He drank.
Then he filled a skin bag with water.
Susanna tied on her sunbonnet.
They walked across the hot prairie.
Terk hadn't been able to go very far.
He lay beside the dry buffalo wallow.
Susanna saw his side move up and down.
"He's alive!" she called and ran to him.
Terk was panting. He didn't open his eyes.

Little Hawk trickled water
onto Terk's tongue.
"He's so hot," Susanna said.
She took off her sunbonnet
and held it to shade the dog's head.
Little Hawk kept giving him water.
"Terk," Susanna coaxed,
"can't you walk as far as the wagon?"
She didn't know what to do.
Then she heard Papa's horse coming.
Papa knew all the waterholes, too.
"Stay and give him water," Papa said.
"I'll bring back the wagon."

Two Indian men returned with Papa.
They helped lift the big dog
into the wagon.
Now Terk opened his eyes
and lifted his head.
He lapped water
from Papa's cupped hands.
"He'll live, won't he?" Susanna asked.
"He'll be all right now," Papa said,
"thanks to you, Little Hawk."
The boy looked happy.
Susanna thanked him, too.
She rode home on the seat beside Papa.
He said, "I'm glad Little Hawk
was the one who found Terk.

Makes White Bull feel better
about accepting water from us."
Susanna smiled.
She knew what Papa meant.
If you did something for a Sioux,
he could hardly wait
to do something for you in return.
"I know why the Indians
won't move into their houses," she said.
"White Bull says
they are square like a box.
Sioux want to live in circles
like their tepees."
Papa said, "Well, if I knew any way
to make a round house
from straight lumber,
I would."
Susanna wished the Indian Agent
could understand Sioux ways
as Papa did.
What would happen the next time
the Agent visited the village
and saw the empty houses?

Chapter 5
Storm

Susanna was wakened in the night
by the shriek of wind.
The windows rattled.
Something heavy struck against the house.
She jumped out of bed.
Papa and Mama were already up.
Mama lighted the kerosene lamp,
then went to comfort Brother.
Papa let Terk into the house.
Susanna shivered at the sudden gust
of icy air
when he opened the door.
"Hail!" Papa said.
He ran to see that the chickens
and cows and horses
were in their shelters.

Big chunks of ice
were pounding the roof
as he returned.
He pushed the door hard
to close it against the wind.
Susanna saw him rub his head.
"Are you hurt?" she asked.

"I'm all right," he said,
"but no man or animal will live long
under that pelting.
Some of that hail
is as big as my fist."
Susanna could scarcely hear him
above the sounds of the storm.
She put her hands over her ears.
She was scared.
Then the rain came.
It poured and poured and poured.
"The clouds have been
saving up all summer
for this one!" Papa said.
Everyone was so happy
that they forgot about
the strong wind and hail
that brought the rain.
Until the next morning.
Susanna stood on the porch with Papa
and looked at the mess the storm had left.
Every leaf was stripped from the bushes.
Every weed and blade of grass
was driven into the muddy earth.

"We were sure lucky
to be in a strong house," she said.
Then she thought of the Indians.
"Papa," she asked,
"wouldn't that wind and hail
ruin the tepees?"
"We'd better ride over
and see what we can do to help," Papa said.
Susanna rode behind the saddle.
She leaned around Papa
so she could see far ahead.
From a distance,
there was nothing on the prairie
except the three square houses.
It looked as if the whole village
had been blown away.
Then, from a small hill,
she saw tepees spread upon the ground.
People moving about.
"They're alive," she said happily.
The Indians were too busy
to pay much attention to them
as they rode into the village.

Women were shaking blankets.
Men were untangling fallen tepees,
spreading them to dry under the sun.
Children were scattered over the prairie,
picking up pots and pans
blown by the wind.
"They've lived through
bad storms before," Papa said.
Susanna knew
that he was as thankful as she was
to find them safe,
but they must have been miserable
the night before.
Then she saw
that White Bull's shelter was gone.
Nothing left, not even the posts.
There was no sign of his tepee.
He was nowhere to be seen.

Papa got off his horse
and lifted her down.
Little Hawk ran to them,
carrying an iron kettle from the prairie.
"Yellow Fur," he called.
"Where's your grandfather?"
Susanna asked.
Little Hawk grinned.
"Come, see," he said.
He took Susanna to the house
Papa had built.

They stood in the opening
where the door had been torn off.
Susanna couldn't believe what she saw.
"Papa," she shouted.
"Come, look!"
For there was White Bull's tepee.
It was set up inside the house,
filling it.
The old man sat in the open door
of the tepee,
dry and comfortable.
"He smelled the storm coming,"
Little Hawk said.
"He moved the tepee inside yesterday."
Susanna saw that Little Hawk
was very proud of his smart grandfather.
She was, too,
but she had to laugh.
Behind her, she heard Papa laughing.
"White Bull found the way
to live in a circle inside a square,"
she said.
"Now the Indians won't be in trouble!"

About the Author

Wilma Pitchford Hays spent her early childhood on a homestead in North Dakota, and her stories of Susanna are drawn from her own experiences. Mrs. Hays is the author of many books for children, including *Siege: The Story of St. Augustine in 1702.* She divides her time between homes in Florida and Connecticut.

About the Artist

Anthony Rao grew up in and around metropolitan New York. After receiving a B.F.A. degree from the Rhode Island School of Design, he worked for a number of years as a staff artist for a children's magazine. Mr. Rao currently lives in New York, where, in addition to illustrating, he also works as an actor.